P9-DIY-172

The MAGNIFICENT MAKERS

Storm Chasers

Go on more
a-MAZE-ing adventures with

The MAGNIFICENT MAKERS

The MAGNIFICENT MAKERS

6

Storm Chasers

by Theanne Griffith
illustrated by Leo Trinidad

A STEPPING STONE BOOK™
Random House 🏠 New York

Text copyright © 2022 by Theanne Griffith
Cover art copyright © 2022 by Reginald Brown
Interior art by Leo Trinidad, inspired by the work of Reginald Brown

All rights reserved. Published in the United States by Random House Children's Books, a division of Penguin Random House LLC, New York.

Random House and the colophon are registered trademarks and A Stepping Stone Book and the colophon are trademarks of Penguin Random House LLC.

Visit us on the Web!
rhcbooks.com

Educators and librarians, for a variety of teaching tools, visit us at
RHTeachersLibrarians.com

Library of Congress Cataloging-in-Publication Data is available upon request
ISBN 978-0-593-56307-6 (trade) — ISBN 978-0-593-56308-3 (lib. bdg.) —
ISBN 978-0-593-56309-0 (ebook)

Printed in the United States of America
10 9 8 7 6 5 4 3 2 1

First Edition

This book has been officially leveled by using
the F&P Text Level Gradient™ Leveling System.

In memory of Mr. Arvin.
I'll always be your second-favorite
third grader! We miss you.
—T.G.

Drip! Drop! Drip!

It was a rainy Monday morning at Newburg Elementary. Dark clouds filled the sky as rain splattered on the ground.

"I wish we could go outside today," said Violet. She rested her chin on her hands as she looked out the foggy window of Mr. Eng's third-grade classroom and sighed.

"I don't mind the rain," replied her best friend, Pablo. "It reminds me of Puerto

Rico and summer storms. I loved playing in my abuela's backyard when it rained. She has this big mango tree. And I would catch the water drops that fell off its leaves in my mouth."

Violet smiled, then looked back out the window. "No mango trees in Newburg," she said. "Just mud and wet grass that I can't play in."

"Well, at least there aren't hurricanes in Newburg. Puerto Rico is beautiful, but sometimes storms turn into hurricanes," Pablo said. "It rains a lot, and the wind blows so fast and strong. Once, my tio's car got blown to the end of his street during a hurricane! He wasn't in it, though."

"Whoa, sounds scary!" Violet replied. "I wonder why Puerto Rico gets them and not Newburg."

"I'm not really sure." Pablo shrugged.

"But my abuela always says it's because the ocean is so warm."

"Hmmmm," Violet thought out loud. "Warm water and hurricanes . . ."

Mr. Eng interrupted her thinking. "Okay, class," he called from the front of the room. "As you can see, we won't be able to go outside today. But . . ." He raised his pencil in the air. "I do have a special surprise for you all."

The students' eyes grew wide. The room hummed with whispers of excitement.

"First, let's go over to the Science Space," Mr. Eng continued.

"Yes!" Violet and Pablo cheered. They stood up with the rest of the class and headed toward the back of the room.

Violet and Pablo were science-loving best friends. One day, Violet was going to be a famous scientist and run her own lab. Pablo loved space and wanted to become an astronaut. But even when they weren't talking about science, Pablo and Violet were always together. They played soccer or double Dutch at recess. They also ate lunch with each other every day. And anytime they were in the Science Space, they worked in the same group.

Today, Violet and Pablo sat down at one of the round tables with the twins, Skylar and Devin. They looked exactly alike. Except Skylar had puffball pigtails, and Devin had a buzz cut with a lightning bolt shaved into the side of his hair.

"I wonder what the surprise is!" Violet said as she sat down.

"I bet it's going to be cool," replied Pablo. "We always do fun stuff in the Science Space."

Skylar nodded and smiled. But Devin just looked at his hands, which were folded in his lap.

Pablo tilted his head and asked, "Are you okay, Devin?"

Devin raised his eyes and offered a small shrug. "Yeah. I was just thinking."

"It's because—" began Skylar.

But Devin interrupted her. "It's okay. I'm fine."

"All right, class," Mr. Eng said. He stood next to a square table. On top of it was a large object covered by a black sheet. "Are you ready for the surprise?"

"Yeah!" the students cheered.

Mr. Eng quickly pulled off the cover. A tall gray box with a clear front door sat on the table. The top part of the box had a fan that faced downward. At the bottom of the box sat a large blue bowl. Mr. Eng smiled proudly. But the room was full of confused faces.

Violet raised her hand. "Mr. Eng, um . . . what is that?"

Mr. Eng tapped the box and said, "This is a tornado machine! This week we are beginning a unit on weather and climate.

And we are going to start off with a demonstration of how tornadoes form."

"That's so cool!" said Skylar.

"That box can make a tornado?" Violet asked.

"I can't wait to see this," added Pablo.

"Yeah, it'll probably be cool," Devin said softly. Skylar put her hand on his shoulder.

"Are you sure you're okay?" asked Violet.

"It's just that our grandpa *always* used to talk about the tornadoes in Oklahoma, and—" said Skylar.

"I'm fine," Devin said again. He took a breath. "I bet the tornado machine will be fun."

Mr. Eng pointed to the blue bowl. "We are going to put dry ice down here. Dry ice is very cold. But when it melts, it doesn't turn into water like regular ice. When dry ice melts, it gives off gas that looks like fog. And we can see it." Mr. Eng pointed at the clear door with his pencil. "To make a tornado, we first turn on the fan. The fan will mix the warmer air from the top of the box with the cold fog from the dry ice below. That mixing of cold and warm air together with the circular winds from the fan should give us a—"

Crackle! Creak! Bam!

A flash of lightning lit up the Newburg sky.

"Tornado," Mr. Eng finished.

"Whoa! Did you see that?" asked Violet.

"It was a huge lightning bolt! Just like the one on the side of your head, Devin."

Devin giggled.

Suddenly, a booming clap of thunder shook the windows and round tables of the Science Space. Without warning, all the lights in the classroom went out.

2

"**U**h-oh," said Mr. Eng. He scratched his head with his pencil. "Well, this changes things a bit." He walked over to the light switch on the wall and flicked it up and down a few times. The classroom stayed dark. Voices whispered with a mix of nervousness and excitement.

Knock! Knock! Knock!

Mr. Eng walked over to the door and opened it. A shadowy figure stood just outside the classroom. It was Mrs. Jenkins, the school principal. She entered with a flashlight in one hand and a box tucked under her other arm.

"Good morning, everyone," she greeted the class. "I'm glad to see that you are all okay. We've lost power, but it should come back in the next ten minutes. It's pretty dark inside, so I'm dropping off flashlights for each classroom." She set the box she was carrying down on a table.

"Thank you, Mrs. Jenkins," Mr. Eng said.

"Thank you!" the class repeated.

"You're most welcome!" Mrs. Jenkins replied as she left the room.

Mr. Eng gave a flashlight to each student. "We'll need to wait for the power to come back to start the tornado machine.

For now, we can go over this handout on the water cycle."

He grabbed a stack of worksheets and passed them out. Violet shined the flashlight on the handout as the group looked it over.

Weather and the Water Cycle

Our atmosphere is full of water. Water moving in and out of the atmosphere is called the **water cycle.** It has a large impact on weather.

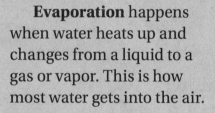

Evaporation happens when water heats up and changes from a liquid to a gas or vapor. This is how most water gets into the air.

Transpiration happens when water vapor is released from plants.

Condensation is when water vapor cools off in the air and forms clouds.

Precipitation is when water returns to the earth as a liquid (rain) or solid (hail/sleet/snow).

"Wow, I didn't know plants give off water," said Skylar.

"Me either," added Violet. "But now that I think about it, I've seen it before!"

Even though it was dark, Violet could see six eyes squinting back at her.

"You've *seen* water—" began Skylar.

"Come *out* of a plant?" finished Devin.

"No way," the twins said together with folded arms.

"I promise! My mom picked some basil from our garden. She sealed it in a plastic bag in the fridge. After a couple of hours it was all steamy! I didn't know how it got like that. But it must have been the water coming out!"

"Ewww!" Skylar giggled. "Sounds like plant sweat."

Devin laughed, too.

Just then, the flashlight Violet was holding went out.

"Oh no!" Pablo moaned.

Violet shook it a few times, and finally the light came back on.

"All okay?" called Mr. Eng from across the room.

"We're fine!" replied Violet.

"Look!" said Skylar suddenly.

The facts on the worksheet had been replaced by a riddle!

"It's from Dr. Crisp!" Violet whispered with excitement. The four friends huddled around the flashlight to read it.

RAIN OR SHINE, SLEET OR SNOW,
WATER IS ALWAYS ON THE GO!
WHAT GOES UP, MUST COME DOWN.
WE CALL IT _____ WHEN
WATER HITS THE GROUND.
BUT BEFORE IT FALLS,
WATER MUST COME TOGETHER.
THAT'S CALLED _____,
A VERY IMPORTANT PART OF WEATHER!
BUT HOW DOES WATER GET
ALL THE WAY UP THERE?
_____ AND
_____ CHANGE IT
FROM LIQUID TO AIR.

SOLVE THIS RIDDLE TO ENTER
THE MAKER MAZE.

"This is a tough one," said Devin.

"Yeah, we barely got a chance to look at the worksheet!" added Skylar.

"It's okay, we can do this," said Violet. She sat up straight in her chair. "I know the last two. *Ee-va-po-RAY-shun*." She sounded out the long word. "Evaporation. And what was that other one?"

"Plant sweat!" Skylar laughed.

"Trans . . . trans—" said Pablo.

"Tran-spi-RAY-shun," Devin mumbled.

"That's it!" said Violet. "Transpiration."

Skylar tried to give Devin two high fives and a fist bump. But he shook his head.

"Okay, we just need the other two," said Pablo, staring at the riddle.

"Pre-cip-i-TAY-shun," Violet said slowly. "I'm pretty sure precipitation is the first one. It's also what the weather woman calls rain!"

"So when water comes together it's called . . . ," Skylar began.

The group was silent until Devin said, "I think that one is *con-den-SAY-shun*."

"That's it! Condensation," Pablo repeated.

In the darkness, the round tables of the Science Space began to tremble. Their chairs bounced, and the flashlight shook in Violet's hand.

"I forgot about this part," said Skylar through chattering teeth.

BOOM! SNAP! WHIZ! ZAP!

3

The shaking suddenly stopped. Violet, Pablo, and the twins glanced around the room. Mr. Eng was frozen while bent over a table explaining the worksheet to a group of students. Another group of students was frozen making funny shadows on the wall with their flashlight. Everyone was still except them and the tornado machine!

"Hey, look over there!" Skylar pointed. The gray box was glowing inside a ring of purple light. And there was a tornado spinning inside!

WHOOOOOOOSH! BIZZAP! WHOOOOOOOSH! BIZZAP!

The fan's spinning blades were pulling the edges of the portal downward.

"I think I liked going through the microscope better," said Skylar. She gulped as she tugged on her ear.

Pablo rubbed his hands together. "Ready?" he asked his friends.

Violet was the first to stand up. "Let's do this!"

Skylar also stood up and grabbed her brother's hand. "Come on, this will be fun! Maybe it will cheer you up."

WHOOOOOOOSH! BIZZAP! WHOOOOOOOSH! BIZZAP!

"It's like the fan is going to suck the

portal into the tornado!" said Skylar as they walked up to the gray box.

"Maybe . . . we should hurry," said Pablo. "Before it *does* suck up the portal. Then we won't be able to get to the Maker Maze!"

Pablo leaned toward the glowing ring of light. But nothing happened.

"Huh," said Violet. She bit her lip. "Maybe we need to open it?" She reached for a small knob on the clear door. The door suddenly flew open! The wind from the tornado machine gushed into the classroom. Worksheets flew everywhere!

"Here we go!" shouted Pablo.

Violet, Pablo, Skylar, and Devin held hands as they were sucked into the portal.

BIZZAP!

After falling for a few moments, they blew into the Maker Maze. Plastic buckets dotted the floor of the main lab. There were long tables that held flasks of colorful bubbling liquid and strange plants that wiggled, jiggled, and danced. Robots were zooming between the lab tables and quickly covering all the equipment with plastic sheets.

"What happened here?" asked Violet as she stood up.

"It looks like a storm came through here, too," said Devin. He dipped his toe in a puddle on the floor.

"My hair's getting wet! It's going to get so frizzy!" Violet complained as she tried to cover her head. Water was leaking everywhere from the Maker Maze ceiling!

"Maybe this will help!" boomed a voice from behind. It was Dr. Crisp! She wore her normal white lab coat and bright purple pants. But this time she also wore yellow rain boots and a yellow umbrella hat!

"Sorry for the mess," said Dr. Crisp. "We had a *little* accident with the storm simulator. It got a bit . . . *too* real. But don't worry! This will all be cleaned up in no time!" She pointed over her shoulder with her thumb. The Maze robots were fixing the ceiling and mopping the floor.

"Anywho!" said Dr. Crisp with a clap of

her hands. She pulled the glittery Maker Manual out from under her lab coat. "Can't get this beauty wet! She'll start to get all frizzy."

"Like my hair!" said Violet. Then she paused and said, "Wait a minute. How can a book get frizzy?"

Dr. Crisp tapped her fingers on the golden cover. "Trust me," she said, shaking her head. "You *don't* want to know."

The Makers giggled as Dr. Crisp smiled and opened the Maker Manual to a page with a large question mark on it.

"So what are we getting ourselves into today?" she asked.

"Well, we were getting ready to learn about weather in the Science Space!" said Skylar.

"Yeah!" agreed Violet and Pablo.

Devin didn't speak but nodded instead.

The pages of the Maker Manual began

to flip. They flipped faster and faster until suddenly stopping on one that read:

LEVEL 1: WHERE DOES THE WATER GO?

Go to door number eleven to begin.

Violet, Pablo, and the twins felt something wrap around their wrists. It was their Magnificent Maker Watches!

"Remember these?" Violet asked Devin and Skylar. "We use them for all kinds of cool stuff to help with each level."

"Yeah! They can even shoot lasers!" added Pablo.

"I definitely remember. But how long do we have to finish the challenge?" asked Skylar. "We barely made it back to class before the portal closed last time!"

"One hundred twenty Maker Minutes," replied Pablo. If they wanted to return to the Maker Maze for more science fun, they had to finish all three levels and make it back through the portal before time was up. If not, they could never come back.

Dr. Crisp snapped the book shut. "Follow me!" She removed her rain boots and umbrella hat, and put on her normal boots and a backpack. Then Dr. Crisp bolted for door number eleven. The Makers followed quickly behind.

"This . . . this . . . It looks like home," said Pablo. The Makers were standing beneath a large palm tree on a long, white sandy beach. In the distance, dark clouds floated over forest-filled mountains. Gentle waves crashed on the shore.

Pablo took a deep breath of salty sea air. "This is Luquillo Beach! In Puerto Rico! I came here all the time with my family when we lived there."

"Pablo, this is beautiful," said Violet, gazing up at the tall trees on the beach.

Devin couldn't help but smile as the sunrays warmed his cheeks.

"I think the Maker Maze knew you needed this," whispered Skylar to her brother.

"Okay, Makers! Listen up," began Dr. Crisp. "This level is all about the water cycle." Then she pressed a button on the side of her watch.

BIZZAP!

Out shot a laser! A purple word appeared in the air. *Condensation.* Dr. Crisp pressed it three more times.

Precipitation.

Evaporation.

Transpiration.

"As you may know, water is *always* moving around in our atmosphere!" she explained, making air waves with her arms and hands. "Sometimes it falls from the sky as rain or snow. And, eventually, water travels back up into the air to make clouds. In level one, you will need to match each word with the stage of the water cycle."

Violet looked toward the rainy mountaintops. "Dr. Crisp, how can we do that? It will take us forever!"

Pablo checked the time with worried eyes. But Dr. Crisp just smiled and yelled into her watch. "Maker Maze, activate jetpacks!"

Without warning, Violet, Pablo, and the twins began to spin. They spun as fast as the tornado back in the Science Space! The beach, ocean, trees, and mountains blurred together. When they stopped, each Maker had a black-and-purple jetpack fastened to their back!

"No way! These are awesome!" Skylar exclaimed.

"With these beauties, you'll be able to complete this level in no time!" said Dr. Crisp.

"This is so cool! I feel like I could blast off into space," Pablo said. He grabbed on to the straps and leaped into the air.

"Just don't press the blue button," replied Dr. Crisp. "Otherwise, you *will* blast off into space!"

The Makers looked at her with dropped jaws and raised eyebrows.

She held her belly and laughed. "I'm just pulling your lab coats," she said. Then she held her three middle fingers down in the shape of an *M*. "Maker's honor! All you have to do is press this purple button. That will activate the jetpacks. Then you grab on to these handles to steer." She pointed to each side of Pablo's jetpack.

Violet grabbed on and bent her knees. "Let's go!" she cheered.

Dr. Crisp smiled. "Okay, but hold your hot plates. There's one more thing." She paused and raised the pencil behind her ear into the air. "You all have to agree where each word goes before you can move it." Then she knelt and opened her backpack. She tossed silver helmets to Violet, Pablo, and the twins. A black *M* was painted on the top of each.

Dr. Crisp lifted her two arms in the air. As she quickly brought them back down, she yelled, "READY! SET! JET!"

VROOOOOOOOOOM!

The Makers' jetpacks fired up. They held tightly to the handles as they flew into the air.

"I thought it was beautiful down there," said Violet, looking at her dangling feet. "But I think it's even more beautiful from here!"

"Sometimes I really miss Puerto Rico," said Pablo. He took a deep breath of salty sea air. "But we should get started."

Violet held on to her jetpack handles and buzzed over to the floating words.

"Which one should we start with?" she asked.

"How about precipitation?" Skylar suggested. "That one is easy. It's when water falls from the sky back to the ground. It goes over there!" She pointed toward the rainy mountaintop.

The group agreed, and Skylar went to grab the word. But her hands passed right through it!

BIZZAP!

"Did we get that wrong?" asked Pablo.

The Makers heard shouting from the beach. It was Dr. Crisp! But they couldn't understand her. She was making a lot of strange motions and movements.

"What do you think she's trying to tell us?" asked Devin.

"It looks like she's walking a fake dog on a leash," said Violet.

"That makes no sense," replied Pablo.

Finally, Dr. Crisp fired up her jetpack and joined them in the air.

"Sorry!" she shouted. "I forgot one small detail. You'll need to use your Magnificent Maker Watches. Press this button and say 'Follow Me!' to move each word. When you've got the word where you want it, press the same button and say 'Stay!'" Then Dr. Crisp zoomed back down and landed on the beach. She gave the Makers two thumbs-up.

Skylar followed Dr. Crisp's directions. Suddenly, the word *precipitation* zoomed over to her side. As Skylar flew to the rainy mountaintop, it followed her! Then she shouted into her watch, "Stay!"

RING, DING, DONG!

"We got it right!" Violet shouted.

Skylar did a happy dance in the air and buzzed back over to her friends.

"Which one should we try next?" asked Pablo.

They studied the three remaining words.

"How about evaporation?" said Violet. "That's how water gets into the air, right?

precipitation

It heats up and turns from a liquid to a *vapor*. E-*vapor*-ate!"

"Yeah! *Vapor* is just another word for *gas,*" Pablo explained.

"That sounds right," the twins agreed.

"I'm going to put it down there," Pablo pointed toward the surface of the ocean. "The sun is probably heating up the water and making it evaporate!" He aimed his watch at the word and hollered, "Follow me!" Then he dove down like a rocket. He stopped right above the gentle waves. Warm sunlight glittered on the surface.

"Stay!" he shouted.

RING, DING, DONG!

Pablo zoomed back up to meet his friends. Dr. Crisp did backflips on the beach as she cheered the Makers on.

"Okay, what about transpiration? Isn't that like evaporation? But the water comes from plants." Violet paused. Then she smiled at Skylar.

"Yeah, plant sweat." Skylar winked.

Pablo and Devin giggled.

Violet pointed with her watch and said, "Follow me!" The word *transpiration* slid through the air toward her. But then she bit her lip. "Where should I put it?" she asked.

"Maybe by one of the palm trees?" Pablo suggested.

Violet zoomed down to the sandy

beach and stood next to one of the large tree trunks.

"Stay!" she shouted into her watch.

But the Maker Maze jingle didn't sound.

She looked back up at her friends. Pablo was pointing to something, but she couldn't tell what. Violet checked her watch. One hundred Maker Minutes to go. She looked back at Pablo. He was pointing to the top of the palm tree.

"Follow me!" she shouted again. She flew up under a wide tree leaf. "Maybe you need to go here," she said to the word *transpiration*. "Stay!"

RING, DING, DONG!

"Yes!" Violet celebrated as she flew back to the group. "I guess plants sweat from their leaves," she joked.

"Okay, the last one is condensation," said Skylar. "You got this one, Devin."

Her brother nodded. "That's when water vapor in the air comes together and turns into clouds." Devin took the word up to a cloud hanging above them.

"Stay!" he shouted into his watch.

RING, DING, DONG!

Devin smiled and launched himself back to the beach toward Dr. Crisp. His friends joined him.

"Magnificent matching!" cheered Dr. Crisp. She gave each Maker a high five.

"Wasn't that fun?" Skylar asked her brother.

"Yeah . . ." He shrugged.

Dr. Crisp got the Maker Manual out of her bag. "Let's see what's next on today's adventure menu!" The book snapped open. The pages blew until stopping on one that read:

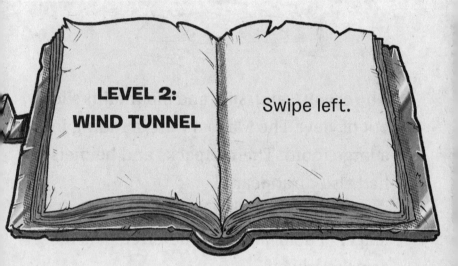

**LEVEL 2:
WIND TUNNEL**

Swipe left.

Dr. Crisp tapped the screen of her watch three times and swiped left. "Hold on!" she shouted.

BIZZAP!

The ocean, sand, sun, and mountains slid out of view. The Makers were standing in a large room. Their jetpacks and helmets had also disappeared.

"I was hoping for another beach challenge," Pablo joked as he stretched his arms overhead.

Violet and Skylar giggled. But Devin just stood next to his sister with his hands in his pockets.

Dr. Crisp suddenly clapped her hands

three times and said, "Okay, Makers! What time is it?" She cupped one hand around her ear.

"It's making time!" Violet and Pablo responded.

"Bingo," said Dr. Crisp with two thumbs-up and a smile. The pages of the Maker Manual flipped again to one with a picture of a weather vane. Below the picture was a list of instructions.

"In this level," Dr. Crisp continued, "you're going to learn about wind. Another very important part of weather! But before we do that, you'll need to make a weather vane!" Dr. Crisp started pulling supplies from her bag. She removed some paper plates, a large straw, a pencil, scissors, a pin, construction paper, and a ball of clay.

"Oh yay!" said Skylar. "We've made

these before, right, Devin?" She gave her brother a nudge with her elbow. "This will definitely be fun."

Devin nodded with a half-smile.

"Are you sure you're okay?" asked Pablo. "You can tell us if something is wrong. We're your friends!"

"I said I was fine," replied Devin. He crossed his arms. "Let's just . . . do this."

Violet looked at Pablo and shrugged.

Dr. Crisp closed her backpack and tossed it toward a corner of the large room. Then she turned toward the Makers with her hands around her mouth.

She shouted, "READY! SET! MAKE!"

The group huddled around the Maker Manual.

"Okay, first we need to cut slits at the end of this straw," said Violet. She reached for the pair of scissors.

"Then we need to cut a small arrow-head for the front," added Pablo. "And a larger one for the tail." He pointed to an outline in the Maker Manual.

"Got it!" replied Violet.

"Let's make the base," Skylar said to her brother, grabbing two paper plates.

"Okay," he agreed. Devin took the modeling clay and flattened it using his hands. Then he smushed it in between the two plates Skylar was holding.

"The base is done!" Skylar called out.

Violet and Pablo worked together to slide the front and tail arrows into the slits in the straw. "We have the top! Let's put them together," Pablo replied.

"You all are *blowing* right through this!" cheered Dr. Crisp. She puffed up her cheeks with air and then pushed it out with her hands.

The Makers laughed. Even Devin.

"Okay, it says that next we have to stick the pencil into the plates through the clay," said Violet as she looked over the instructions.

Pablo grabbed the pencil and jammed it point-down through the plates. "Now we need to use the pin to connect the vane to the pencil's eraser."

When they finished, the Maker Maze jingle echoed throughout the room.

RING, DING, DONG!

"Flippin' funnel clouds! You all finished fast!" hollered Dr. Crisp.

Violet went to give double high fives to everyone . . . except Devin shook his head.

"Oh, Devin, come on!" Violet insisted. "Why did you come if you didn't want to have fun!"

"Hey!" said Skylar. Her forehead wrinkled as she said, "Leave him alone. He doesn't have to high-five if he doesn't want to."

"Skylar's right, Violet," said Pablo.

"No. Violet's right," Devin said. "I'm

not sure why I came." His chest sunk and he lowered his head. "I'm just going to sit over here."

Dr. Crisp frowned and removed the pencil from her ear. She used it to scratch her chin before asking, "Did I miss something? Is everyone okay?"

Skylar looked at her brother, who was leaning against the wall. She paused before saying, "Devin will be okay. I think he needs some space."

"Can you just tell us?" asked Violet.

"Devin asked me not to say anything, so I won't," replied Skylar. She put a hand on her hip.

Pablo checked his watch again. "If Devin wants to sit out this level or the whole challenge, that's fine. But we need to keep going if we want to finish on time."

Dr. Crisp looked over her shoulder at Devin. "We won't go on without you, Devin. Unless you say it's okay."

Devin responded with a head nod.

Dr. Crisp replied with a salute.

"Okay, then. Hold on!" She shouted into her watch. "Maker Maze, activate wind tunnel!"

BOOM! SNAP! WHIZ! ZAP!

7

A flood of purple fog filled the room. When it cleared, a long table with two large black boxes were in front of the Makers. They were open on the top and each had a purple *M* drawn on the side. They were connected by a long clear tube.

"Listen up, Makers!" began Dr. Crisp. "It's time to put that weather vane to use and figure out"—she paused and stuck her pointer finger in the air—"which way the wind blows. And why!"

"How are we going to do *that* with

those boxes?" asked Pablo, pointing to the strange setup.

"That's what you'll—" began Dr. Crisp.

"Have to figure out!" Violet and Skylar finished together.

Dr. Crisp laughed and said, "It's going to be a *breeze*!" Then she leaped into the air with her fist high and said, "READY! SET! THINK!"

Violet, Pablo, and Skylar explored the two boxes.

"I don't understand what is going on. Where's the wind?" Skylar wondered. She lifted her palm faceup. The air in the room was still.

"Me either," said Pablo. He scratched his cheek.

Violet bit her lip and thought for a moment. She went over to one box and stuck her hand in. "Brrrrrr!" she said,

bringing it
back out quickly.
"That's cold! But I didn't
feel any wind."

"Maybe we're missing something," said Pablo. He circled
the table, looking at every corner. But he
was stumped. "This is the strangest challenge ever. How can we learn about wind
when there isn't any?" he mumbled.

Dr. Crisp walked around the room, whistling with her hands folded behind her back.

"We can do this," Violet said. She went back over to the same box and stuck her hand in again. She shivered as she removed it.

"Look at the goose bumps on your arm!" said Skylar.

"I know! I told you it was super cold. Try it!" Violet replied. She rubbed her arms quickly with her palms.

Both Pablo and Skylar stuck their hands inside.

"Oh wow! That *is* super cold!" said Pablo.

Then Violet hurried over to the other box. She slowly put her hand inside. *"Aaaaaaah,"* she said. "This one is nice and toasty."

Pablo and Skylar put their hands in, too.

"So . . . one box is freezing, and the other is warm," said Skylar. She looked over at her brother. He watched them work with his chin in his hands.

"Wait!" said Pablo suddenly. "The weather vane! We should use it to track down the wind!"

"Beep! Beep! Beep!" Dr. Crisp held her arms together and pretended to scan the floor with a metal detector.

"You're right, Pablo," Violet agreed. "We got so distracted by the boxes that we forgot to use the tool we made!" Violet picked up the weather vane and paused. "Now what?"

"I bet wind is blowing through that tunnel. Why else would it be there?" Skylar suggested.

"Let's find out!" Violet reached into the warm box and placed the weather vane near the tunnel's exit hole.

"Look!" said Pablo, peering over the top of the box. "It's starting to move!"

"That's so cool!" said Skylar. "There *is* some wind here!"

"Yeah, but how?" Violet wondered.

"Not sure, but we have to figure it out soon," Pablo reminded the group. "We only have fifty Maker Minutes left to finish this level *and* level three!"

50 min. left

"It's okay. There's time," said Violet.

"What happens if we move the weather vane to the other side of the tunnel?"

She tested her idea.

Nothing happened. The straw didn't spin!

"Wait, so it spins on the warm side, but not on the cold side?" Pablo placed his two palms on his forehead. "I'm so confused," he moaned.

"It has something to do with temperature," said Skylar as she tapped her chin. "Oh! And Mr. Eng said something about cold and warm air when he was setting up the tornado machine!" She looked back toward her brother. "I bet Devin knows. He and my grandpa talked about this stuff all the time."

"Then why won't he help us?" Pablo sighed.

"It's not that. Just give me a sec," Skylar

replied. She hurried over to her brother and bent down. She whispered something in his ear. Then she gave him a hug.

A few moments later, both Devin and Skylar walked back over to Violet and Pablo.

"Warm air rises and cold air sinks!" Skylar blurted out.

Violet and Pablo exchanged glances.

"What does that have to do with wind?" asked Pablo.

Devin took a breath before replying. "When warm air rises, it makes room for the cold air to come in. That's how wind is created. And that's why the weather vane only moves on the warm side of the tunnel. Because the cold air is moving in to replace the warm air."

RING, DING, DONG!

"Yeah!" Everyone cheered.

Except for Devin. He let out another big breath and started to sniffle.

8

"**W**hat a whirlwind!" hollered Dr. Crisp as she joined the Makers. "Great . . . job?" She paused as she saw Devin wipe a small tear from the corner of his eye. "No need to be sad. You all figured it out! And there's still plenty of time to finish the challenge!" Dr. Crisp explained, showing everyone her watch.

Devin was quiet for a moment before finally replying. "I'm trying to be happy. I promise. But it's really hard." He sighed. "One year ago, today . . . my grandpa died. There. I said it." His sister gave him a one-armed hug. "He was my best friend. Besides Skylar."

Violet's eyes softened. "Oh, Devin, I'm so sorry. We had no idea."

"He had a farm in Oklahoma," he replied. "And when I visited, we always talked about the weather."

Skylar nodded. "The weather is really important to farmers," she said.

"That's how I learned about wind," Devin continued. "But now he's gone." He hung his head again.

Dr. Crisp knelt in front of him. "Can I tell you a sort-of secret?" she asked.

Devin wiped another tear and nodded.

"I also cry sometimes when I think of my grandpa. He was my best friend, too. I called him Paw-Paw Crispy!"

Devin giggled.

"He taught me everything I needed to know to run the Maker Maze," Dr. Crisp continued. "He's gone now, too. But I still miss him and think about him often."

"You still get sad when you think about him?" asked Devin.

"Sometimes I do. And other times I feel happy. Our feelings are kind of like the weather. Some days are sunny and other days are stormy. And that's okay."

"I definitely feel stormy today," replied Devin. "But talking with you makes me feel better. A little more sunny." Devin smiled and wrapped his arms around Dr. Crisp's neck and gave her a hug. "Thank you."

"You're most welcome, Devin," Dr. Crisp replied.

Then Devin held his head high. "My grandpa wouldn't want me to be sad." He rubbed his hands together and looked at his friends. "Let's do this!"

Dr. Crisp gave Devin another salute. "Aye, aye, captain!" She found her backpack and opened it. She pulled out the Maker Manual, which flew open to a page that read:

LEVEL 3: SPINNING STORMS

Go through tunnel L.

Dr. Crisp packed away the glittery golden book, then yelled into her watch, "Maker Maze, open sesame!"

The Makers waited. But nothing happened.

"Hmmmm," said Dr. Crisp, scratching her head with her pencil. "Maybe I forgot the password."

"But, Dr. Crisp, we only have thirty Maker Minutes left!" Pablo said, grabbing his cheeks.

30 min. left

"Aha! I remember now," Dr. Crisp replied. "Maker Maze, open *supercell*!"

Just then, a circle opened in the ceiling. The Makers gazed up. It was dark, but they could hear a soft wind howling from above.

"Ready?" Dr. Crisp asked with a big smile. Then she leaped into the air.

BIZZAP!

"See you all *sooooon*!" Her voice trailed into the darkness.

"What are you waiting for?" asked Violet. "Come on!" She also jumped into the air and was sucked into the wind tunnel. Pablo and the twins followed.

BIZZAP!

After many twists and turns, and one really sharp corner, the Makers landed in another large room. Violet grabbed the sides of her head with both hands. Her eyes still felt like they were moving.

"I'm dizzy," she said.

"All righty, folks!" shouted Dr. Crisp from the other side of the room. "It's time for the last level of the challenge." Then she called into her watch, "Maker Maze, activate weather boxes!"

The floor began to tremble beneath the Makers' feet.

"Wait, I'm still spinning," said Devin. His voice wobbled with the rest of the room.

BOOM! SNAP! WHIZ! ZAP!

A blast of purple light filled the room. When it faded, two huge see-through boxes came into view. They were twice as tall as Dr. Crisp and extra wide! One was partly filled with water. The other had a layer of dirt covering the bottom. Both had what looked like dark storm clouds floating near the top!

"Okay, Makers! Listen up!" Dr. Crisp walked in between the two giant boxes. "In this box," she said, tapping the one with water, "a hurricane will form!"

Pablo's eyes grew wide. "It's going to stay in the box, though, right? I've been in a hurricane back in Puerto Rico. It was . . . scary."

Dr. Crisp smiled and signed. "Maker's honor!" Then she continued. "And in this box, a tornado will touch down! It will be your job to figure out three ways tornadoes and hurricanes are the same," Dr. Crisp explained, holding up three fingers. "AND . . . three ways they are different." She held up three fingers on her other hand. "Use your watches to record your answers." Dr. Crisp pointed to one of the buttons on the side of her watch.

Violet asked the twins, "Did you ever see a tornado at your grandpa's farm in Oklahoma?"

They shook their heads.

"But he told me *all* about them," replied

71

Devin. He straightened up and stood tall. With hands on his hips and a smile on his face, he said, "We've got this. Ready when you are, Dr. Crisp!"

Dr. Crisp shouted into her watch, "Maker Maze, activate spinning storms!"

BOOM! SNAP! WHIZ! ZAP!

The storm boxes began to shake.

CRACK! CRASH! BAM!

Thunderclaps echoed throughout the room. The dark storm clouds floating at the top of the boxes began to move. Dr. Crisp cupped her hands around her mouth and screamed, "READY! SET! BRAINSTORM!"

The Makers slowly approached the boxes. Wind was picking up in both. The storm clouds began to move in a circular motion. Waves started to crash into the sides of the hurricane box. In the tornado box, a funnel cloud dropped until it finally touched down. Dust flew in the air!

"Okay, let's think about this," Violet said. "There are some things that are definitely different between tornadoes and hurricanes."

"And some that are definitely the same," added Skylar. "Both hurricanes and tornadoes have really strong winds! It probably has something to do with air temperature."

"You're getting *warmer*!" cheered Dr. Crisp.

"Tornadoes form when cold air from the north runs into the warm air from the south," Devin explained. "That's why you get so many in the middle of the country!"

"I bet it's the same for hurricanes!" said Violet. "Isn't that what your abuela said, Pablo?"

"You're right! She said Puerto Rico gets hurricanes because of the warm water!" replied Pablo, rubbing his hands together.

"Warm water *evaporates* from the ocean. It becomes warm air and rises to the sky," Skylar said. "We learned that in level one! And in level two—"

"We learned that cold air replaces warm air to create wind!" Devin finished. "I bet when it happens over and over, it can cause a storm! Like a hurricane or a tornado!"

"That's it!" said Violet. She hollered into her watch, "Both tornadoes and hurricanes form because warm and cold air mix to create strong spinning winds!"

((((((((RING, DING, DONG!))))))))

"Way to *warm up*!" cheered Dr. Crisp.

Pablo continued to examine the storm boxes. Then he said, "I know a difference!" He lifted his watch to his mouth and said, "Hurricanes form over water, but tornadoes form over land!"

((((((((RING, DING, DONG!))))))))

"I got one, too!" said Devin. "Tornadoes touch the ground because the wind makes a funnel!" He pointed to the long funnel cloud in the tornado box. "Hurricanes don't do this. They stay in the air."

RING, DING, DONG!

"And aren't hurricanes way bigger than tornadoes?" asked Skylar.

"They kind of look the same size here," Violet pointed out.

"No, hurricanes in real life are huge!" said Pablo. "The hurricane I was in a couple of years ago was as big as Puerto Rico itself!"

"Yeah, tornadoes can get big. But not *that* big," replied Devin.

RING, DING, DONG!

"Yes! We figured out three differences!" Violet jumped up and down.

"But we still have to figure out two more similarities. And we only have eight Maker Minutes left!" Pablo exclaimed.

"It's okay. We are almost there! We just have to think harder," Violet said.

But the Makers were stuck.

"Wait!" Devin suddenly blurted. "I think I got one."

Violet, Pablo, and Skylar listened with eager ears.

"My grandpa told me once that when he was a little boy, a huge tornado passed over his farm. It destroyed *everything*," Devin explained.

"Oh yeah, I remember this story," said Skylar. "They just barely made it to the storm shelter!"

"Yeah! And he said before his dad could close the door, it flew open," Devin continued. "Everyone was so scared. But as the tornado went over them, there was a calm part. A part without much wind."

"Wait a minute!" said Pablo with a big smile. "Hurricanes have those, too! It's called the *eye*!"

Devin shouted the answer into his watch.

RING, DING, DONG!

"We did it!" said Violet as she gave Devin a high five. "Your grandpa taught you so much!"

Devin smiled softly. "He sure did," he said.

Then Dr. Crisp ran over with her watch in the air. It was flashing purple!

"Uh-oh!" said Violet.

"Sorry to burst your blimp, Makers. But we only have three minutes left!"

3 min. left

"**W**hy does this always happen!" Pablo pulled his cheeks with his hands.

"No time to panic, Pablo," said Violet. "We need to think. Fast!"

Skylar held up her pointer finger. "We need to think of *one* more thing that tornadoes and hurricanes have in common," she said.

The Makers ran around the storm boxes and studied them carefully.

"We need to hurry!" Devin shouted.

"I got it!" said Violet suddenly. "Devin

and Skylar, you just said a tornado destroyed your grandpa's farm when he was young."

The twins nodded.

"And, Pablo," Violet said, turning toward her best friend. "You said that you were in a hurricane before."

Pablo also nodded. "Yup, Hurricane Maria. It was awful! It—" Then Pablo gasped. A smile crept onto his face. "It destroyed so much!"

"That's it!" Devin and Skylar said.

Violet shouted into her watch, "Both hurricanes and tornadoes can cause a lot of damage!"

(((((RING, DING, DONG!)))))

"Thumpin' thunderclouds! You all did it!" cheered Dr. Crisp.

But there was no time to celebrate.

"We only have one minute left!" cried Pablo with his wrist in the air.

"You all know what that means!" Dr. Crisp replied. "Time to catch a tailwind on out of here!" She sprinted to the door.

The Makers followed closely behind.

"We're at door number twenty!" shouted Skylar. "We need to—"

"RUN!" Devin screamed.

Dr. Crisp and the Makers sprinted down the long hallway lined with doors.

"Ten seconds!" Dr. Crisp shouted as she ran into the main lab.

Violet, Pablo, Devin, and Skylar ran under the portal. It was slowly starting to close.

They grabbed hands and jumped as high as they could.

BIZZAP!

They flew out of the tornado machine and landed in front of the square table in the Science Space. One second later, the lights came on in the room, and everyone unfroze.

"Well, it looks like the electricity is back on," said Mr. Eng. Then he saw Violet, Pablo, and the twins on the floor.

"What's going on here?" he asked.

"Um . . ." Pablo stumbled as he got up.

"We were just . . . ," began Devin.

"Trying to find . . . ," continued Skylar.

"Our worksheet!" said Violet. Several worksheets had scattered onto the floor when the portal first opened. She held one up for Mr. Eng to see. "It fell on the floor and . . . it was too dark to find it."

Mr. Eng squinted at the group of friends. "Okay, well, dust yourselves off and have a seat, please."

They quickly stood up and went back to their table.

"Hey, you have dirt on your shirt," said Pablo. He brushed Violet's shoulder.

"You do, too," said Skylar to her brother.

"We all do," replied Devin in a hushed voice. "It must be the dust from the tornado box back in the Maker Maze!"

"It did get everywhere," added Violet.

They quickly shook themselves off.

Then Mr. Eng came over to their table. He squatted in front of them. "Now, I know you all really love science. But it's important to stay in your seats when we have emergencies. It's for your own safety."

"We're sorry, Mr. Eng," said Pablo.

Mr. Eng smiled. "No problem. Just a

reminder." He grasped the table as he stood up.

When he walked away, Violet nudged Pablo.

"Look!" She pointed at the table. "Mr. Eng left behind dusty fingerprints!"

"How did *he* get all dusty, too?" Pablo scratched his cheek.

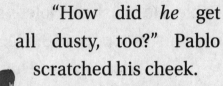

"Do you think...," Skylar began.

"He followed us to the Maker Maze?" Devin finished.

The four friends exchanged funny looks.

"Nah!"

Make your own creations!

⋛ MAKE A WEATHER VANE! ⋚

Always *make* carefully and with adult supervision!

MATERIALS

1 ball of modeling clay
1 pin
1 straw
2 paper plates (two pieces of
    cardboard also works!)
construction paper
markers
pencil with an eraser
scissors

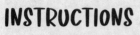

INSTRUCTIONS

1. Use markers to write *north, south, east,* and *west* on one of the paper plates. Get creative! Use extra markers to decorate the plates!

2. Cut a small slit on each side of one end of the straw. Do the same for the other end.

3. Cut a triangle and a trapezoid out of the construction paper. Then insert them into the small slits in the straw. The triangle will be used as the arrowhead, and the trapezoid will form the arrow's tail.

TRIANGLE

TRAPEZOID

4. Roll your modeling clay into a ball and place it in between your paper plates. Flatten, then stick the pencil point through the top plate and into the clay.

5. Use a pin to attach the straw into the eraser of the pencil.

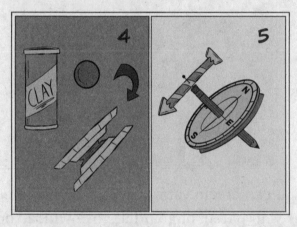

6. Go outside and observe! You can use a compass application on a smart device, like a cell phone or tablet, to figure out which direction is north.

7. Which way is the wind blowing? Write down your findings. You can do this each day for a week, or even for a whole month, to track the wind patterns!*

*You can create your own experiment sheet or ask your parent or guardian to download one at theannegriffith.com.

Your parent or guardian can share pictures and videos of your weather vane on social media using #MagnificentMakers.

≋ MAKE A MINI WATER CYCLE! ≋

MATERIALS

1 large rubber band or piece
of string
clear plastic wrap
large bowl
mug
pitcher or bucket
water

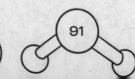

INSTRUCTIONS

1. Put the bowl in a sunny place outside.
2. Pour water into the bowl using a pitcher or bucket. You can also use a hose!
3. Carefully place the mug in the center of the bowl. Try not to let any water inside of it.

4. Cover the top of the bowl tightly with plastic wrap. Use a large rubber band to secure the plastic wrap. You can also tie a piece of string around the bowl to hold the plastic wrap in place.

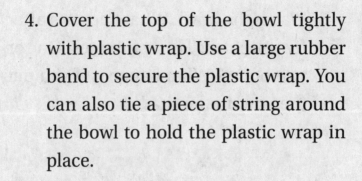

93

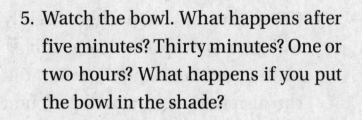

5. Watch the bowl. What happens after five minutes? Thirty minutes? One or two hours? What happens if you put the bowl in the shade?

6. Watch the water cycle in action! Record your observations.*

*You can create your own experiment sheet or ask your parent or guardian to download one at theannegriffith.com.

You should be able to see water droplets form on the top of the plastic wrap. This is because the water evaporates from the bowl. Eventually, when the droplets are heavy enough, they will fall back down and into the mug! Figure out how long this takes to happen. What makes the water cycle go faster? How long does it take to collect an inch of water in the mug? Ask questions and get creative!

Your parent or guardian can share pictures and videos of your mini water cycle on social media using #MagnificentMakers.

Missing the
Maker Maze already?

Read on for a peek at the Magnificent Makers' next adventure!

The trembling stopped and everything was still. This happened each time the portal to the Maker Maze opened. Now Violet and Pablo just had to find the ring of purple light that would actually send them to the Maker Maze.

"What is going on?" squeaked a voice.

Violet and Pablo turned to see who it was. Lorenzo was looking around the room at his frozen friends. His hands were gripping his desk so tightly his knuckles had turned white.

"Yay! You're coming with us!" said Violet.

"Where?" asked Lorenzo with a confused face.

"The Maker Maze!" Violet and Pablo responded.

Lorenzo looked like he wanted to ask another question. Before he could, Violet said, "You'll see when we get there."

"But first, we need to find the portal," added Pablo. He saw a purple light out of the corner of his eye. "This way!" he shouted.

The friends hurried over behind Mr. Eng's desk. Their teacher was frozen in front of the class with his finger in the air.

"Excuse me, Mr. Eng," Violet joked.

Laying on the floor was the model

human body. Glowing around it was a ring of purple light.

"Cool! Are we in a video game or something?" asked Lorenzo.

Violet and Pablo laughed. "The Maker Maze is better than *any* game out there," replied Pablo. He put his three middle fingers down and said, "Maker's honor."

"Cool. I still don't get what the Maker Maze is, but it sounds like fun!" Lorenzo exclaimed. Then he bent over to get a better look at the ring of light. "So how exactly do we get—" Lorenzo didn't finish his sentence.

BIZZAP!

He was sucked into the portal! Pablo and Violet jumped in after him.

BIZZAP!

The Makers fell through the darkness

for a few seconds before landing on the floor of the Maker Maze.

"Ahhh, feels good to be back!" said Violet, stretching her hands over her head.

"You weren't kidding. This *is* better than a video game!" said Lorenzo.

Violet and Pablo gave Lorenzo a quick tour while they waited for Dr. Crisp to show up. They led him down the long lab tables that housed strange plants, creepy bugs, and flasks filled with colorful bubbling liquids. Pablo pointed out his favorite gadget: the zero gravity chambers. Then Violet showed Lorenzo the large microscope. That was her favorite.

"We go through one of those doors to start the challenge," explained Pablo. He peered down a long hallway lined with doors.

Lorenzo squinted. It was so long he couldn't see where it ended. "Whoa, that's a lot of doors."

"Each challenge has three levels," added Violet. "We need to finish the challenge in one hundred twenty Maker Minutes. That's when they unfreeze," she said, showing Lorenzo a screen above them. Their classmates back in Newburg Elementary were still frozen in place.

"And we can't come back to the Maker Maze if we don't finish in time," said Pablo.

Lorenzo smiled. "I love a good challenge! Just like wrestling. Game on!" he cheered with fists in the air.

"We need to find Dr. Crisp first," Violet began. "She runs this place."

"And goes with us on the challenge," added Pablo.

"What's shakin', Makers?" hollered a voice from behind.

It was Dr. Crisp! She removed some stained gloves from her hands and tossed them on the floor next to her backpack. She had a black oil smudge on her forehead.

"Sorry I'm late! One of the robots got sick, so I was doing some repairs. Hey there, Lorenzo! Cool cast!" said Dr. Crisp.

"I broke my arm wrestling," he replied slowly. He gazed up at the rainbow-haired scientist in purple pants standing in front of him. "Wait," he said. "How do you know my name?"

Dr. Crisp reached for a backpack sitting on one of the long lab tables. She pulled out the glittery golden Maker Manual.

"This gal knows it all!" she replied.

"And she tells me everything." Dr. Crisp winked. "So, Makers. What are you in the mood to learn today?" She opened the book to a page with a giant question mark on it.

"The human body!" Violet and Pablo shouted.

The pages began to turn with increasing speed. They flipped faster and faster until they came to a very sudden stop on a page that read:

**LEVEL 1:
GO WITH
THE FLOW**

Enter
through door
number eight.

Dr. Crisp snapped the book shut and tossed it into her backpack. She knelt to look Violet, Pablo, and Lorenzo in the eyes. "Who's with me?"

"We are!" the Makers replied.

"Thumpin' thermometers! That's what I like to hear!" Dr. Crisp turned and stomped with high knees down the never-ending hallway.

As the Makers followed, Magnificent Maker Watches appeared on their wrists.

"Oh cool! What's this?" asked Lorenzo.

"I'll explain in a second. We should go!" said Pablo.

The Makers chased behind Dr. Crisp until arriving at door number eight. Their watches glowed and vibrated as they entered. The challenge had begun.

Acknowledgments

Thank you for being an amazing partner, Jorge. Writing this series wouldn't be so easy or fun without you in my corner. Mom and Dad, thank you for always teaching me to love reading and writing. I love you, Dad, and I love and miss you immensely, Mom. To my beautiful daughters, Violeta and Lila, you inspire me every day. Thank you for being exactly who you are. I love watching you grow into little curious ladies. I hope these books make you proud. To my best friend, Stephanie, thank you for allowing me to include memories of your dad in this book. He is very missed. To the entire Random House team, Caroline Abbey, Tricia Lin, Lili Feinberg, Kimberly Small, and countless others, thank you! I am so lucky to be a part of such a talented and hardworking team. Finally, I'd like to thank my amazing agent, Chelsea Eberly. You're the best! Thank you for your continued guidance and support.